My Dog
Is an Elephant

Text by Rémy Simard
Illustrated by Pierre Pratt

Annick Press Ltd.
Toronto • New York

© 1994 Rémy Simard (text)
© 1994 Pierre Pratt (art)
Design by Jeffrey Rosenberg
English adaptation by David Homel.

Annick Press Ltd.

Annick Press gratefully acknowledges the support of the Canada Council and the Ontario Arts Council.

Canadian Cataloguing in Publication Data

Simard, Rémy
My Dog is an Elephant

ISBN 1-55037-977-1 (bound)
ISBN 1-55037-976-3 (pbk)

I. Pratt, Pierre II. Title.

PS8587.I53M8 1994 JC813'.54 C94-930731-9
PZ7.S56My 1994

The art in this book was rendered in inks and acrylics.
The text was typeset in Garamond, 22 and 32 point.

Distributed in Canada by:
Firefly Books Ltd.
250 Sparks Avenue
Willowdale, Ontario M2H 2S4

Published in the U.S.A. by Annick Press (U.S.) Ltd.
Distributed in the U.S.A. by:
Firefly Books (U.S.) Inc.
P.O. Box1338
Ellicot Station
Buffalo, NY 14205

Printed on acid-free paper.
Printed and bound in Canada by:
D.W. Friesen & Sons, Altona, Manitoba

Every Tuesday morning,
Hector would go off to play
in his sandbox.

But this week,
an unexpected guest
was waiting
for him.

"Hey, Elephant! What are
you doing in my sandbox?"
"I ran away from the zoo,"
the frightened elephant told him,
"and now they're looking for me
everywhere. If they catch me,
they'll throw me in jail. And
I didn't even steal anything!"
And the elephant began to cry.

"There, there," Hector said to
the elephant. "If you don't stop
crying, we'll both drown. I'll help
you hide."

Hector brought the elephant up to his little bedroom; he was sure no one would discover him there. Except for his mother. "An elephant!" she screamed, then fainted dead away. Bang !

"Quick," Hector said to his friend, "you have to hide before my mother wakes up."

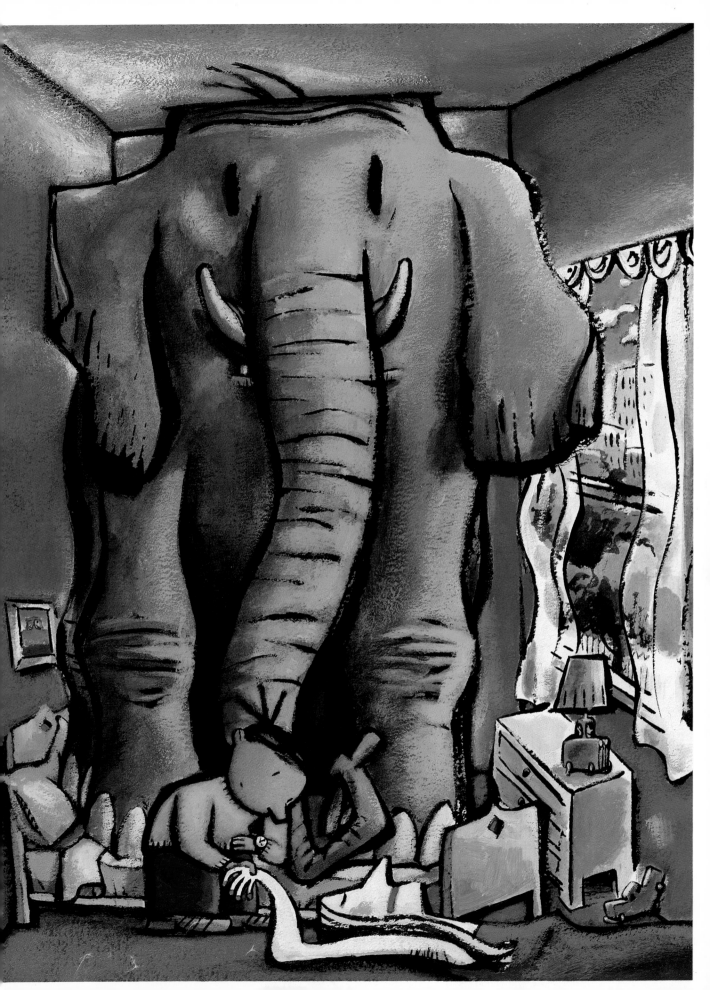

By the time she woke up, the
elephant had disappeared. But he kept
showing up in the strangest places...

She opened the dresser drawer... Bang !

She looked under the bed... Bang !

She opened the closet... Bang !

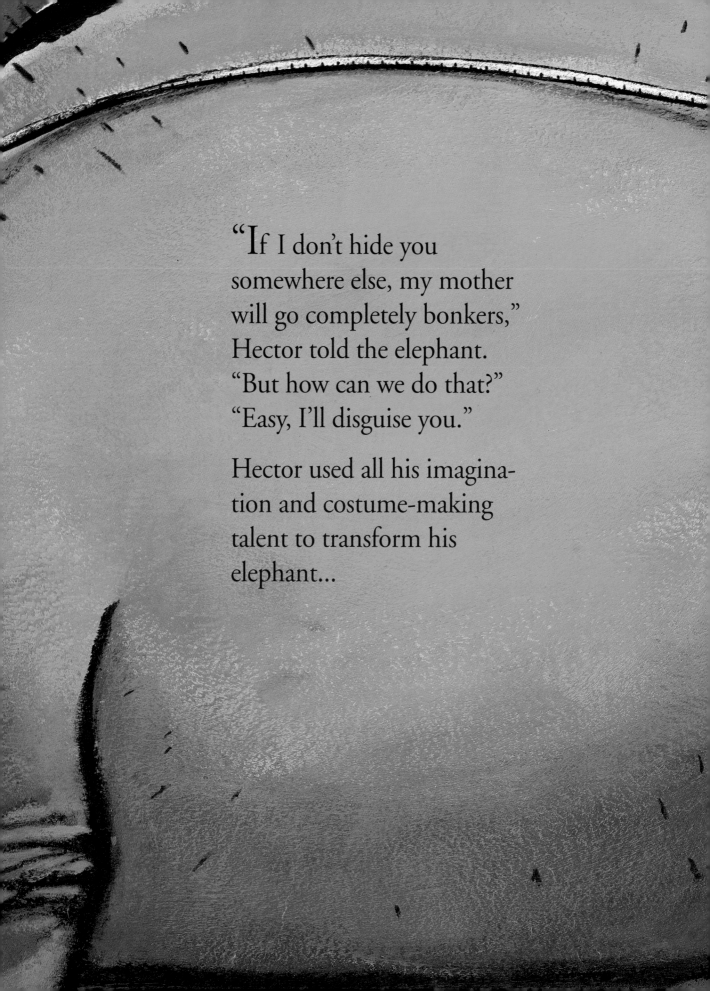

"If I don't hide you
somewhere else, my mother
will go completely bonkers,"
Hector told the elephant.
"But how can we do that?"
"Easy, I'll disguise you."

Hector used all his imagina-
tion and costume-making
talent to transform his
elephant...

Hector was very proud of himself, but he didn't know that it was open season on moose.

When he realized that, Hector picked a new disguise for his elephant.

But there was one little problem: dinosaurs had disappeared a long time ago. When they stepped into the street, they were besieged by thousands of scientists in lab jackets.

So Hector disguised
his elephant as a butterfly.
But there was one little
problem: he never imagined
a butterfly of this size would
attract so many collectors.

But Hector wasn't
discouraged. He decided to
use his costume from last
Hallowe'en. The elephant
took it and slipped it on,
which was no small bit of
business.

Once it was on,
Hector went out to walk
his new dog.

To make sure no one suspected
the truth, he told his elephant what
a dog was expected to do.

He has to bark:

Woof !

Bring the
newspaper...
without
the paperboy.

And
lift his leg
on the fire
hydrant.

Everything was working out fine. The elephant was enjoying his dog's life. But one day, what had to happen happened: Rip! The little costume was in shreds.

Hector was discovering that camouflaging an elephant is a big business. He decided to help him return to his country, somewhere in Africa. He took his piggy bank and went to buy an airplane ticket as big as his large friend.

Back at the house, he lent his father's suit to his elephant. "I'll have to tell Papa to go on a diet. His clothes fit you like a glove."

Together they went to the airport.
Hector wished his friend a pleasant journey.
The elephant went through customs and
turned around to wave goodbye.
"I'll write," he called to Hector, as he
prepared to get on the plane.

Hector went back home.
He was a little sad
at having lost his big friend.

But there is a surprise
waiting for him...

He heard a little voice.
"Help me, help me ! There are way
too many cats around here."

"Come with me," Hector told him.
"There are no cats in my room."

Delicately, Hector picked
up the mouse and brought
him back home.
"It's very nice of you to help
me hide, but there's one thing
I must tell you..."

And just as the mouse took
off his big ears, Hector's
mother opened the door to his
room and came face to face
                              with...